AHS 6244
19.95
m-35

**SPORTS INJURIES:
HOW TO PREVENT, DIAGNOSE, & TREAT**

ICE SKATING

Sports Injuries:
How to Prevent, Diagnose, & Treat

- Baseball
- Basketball
- Cheerleading
- Equestrian
- Extreme Sports
- Field
- Field Hockey
- Football
- Gymnastics
- Hockey
- Ice Skating
- Lacrosse
- Soccer
- Track
- Volleyball
- Weight Training
- Wrestling

SPORTS INJURIES:
HOW TO PREVENT, DIAGNOSE, & TREAT

ICE SKATING

MICHAEL STREETER

MASON CREST PUBLISHERS
www.masoncrest.com

Mason Crest Publishers Inc.
370 Reed Road
Broomall, PA 19008
(866) MCP-BOOK (toll free)
www.masoncrest.com

Copyright © 2004 Mason Crest Publishers, Inc.

All rights reserved. No part of this publication may be reproduced or transmitted in any form or by any means, electronic or mechanical, including photocopying, recording, taping, or any information storage and retrieval system, without permission in writing from the publisher.

First printing

1 2 3 4 5 6 7 8 9 10

Library of Congress Cataloging-in-Publication Data on file
at the Library of Congress

ISBN 1-59084-635-4

Series ISBN 1-59084-625-7

Editorial and design by
Amber Books Ltd.
Bradley's Close
74–77 White Lion Street
London N1 9PF
www.amberbooks.co.uk

Project Editor: Michael Spilling
Design: Graham Curd
Picture Research: Natasha Jones

Printed and bound in the Hashemite Kingdom of Jordan

PICTURE CREDITS
Corbis: 6, 8, 11, 12, 13, 15, 17, 18, 22, 23, 24, 25, 26, 28, 33, 36, 38, 40, 43, 50, 51, 52, 54, 55, 59; **©EMPICS**: 20, 44; **POPPERFOTO**: 57.

FRONT COVER: Corbis (tl, br); ©EMPICS (bl, tr).

ILLUSTRATIONS: Courtesy of Amber Books except:
Bright Star Publishing plc: 48, 49;
Tony Randell: 29, 30, 31.

IMPORTANT NOTICE

This book is intended to provide general information about sports injuries, their prevention, and their treatment. The information contained herein is not intended as a substitute for professional medical care. Always consult a doctor before beginning any exercise program, and for diagnosis and treatment of any injury. Accordingly, the publisher cannot accept any responsibility for any prosecution or proceedings brought or instituted against any person or body as a result of the use or misuse of the techniques and information within.

CONTENTS

Foreword	6
History	8
Mental Preparation to Avoid Injury	18
Warming Up to Avoid Injury	26
Equipment	36
Common Injuries and Treatment	44
Careers in Skating	52
Glossary	60
Further Information	62
Index	64

Foreword

Sports Injuries: How to Prevent, Diagnose, and Treat is a seventeen-volume series written for young people who are interested in learning about various sports and how to participate in them safely. Each volume examines the history of the sport and the rules of play; it also acts as a guide for prevention and treatment of injuries, and includes instruction on stretching, warming up, and strength training, all of which can help players avoid the most common musculoskeletal injuries. *Sports Injuries* offers ways for readers to improve their performance and gain more enjoyment from playing sports, and young athletes will find these volumes informative and helpful in their pursuit of excellence.

Sports medicine professionals assigned to a sport that they are not familiar with can also benefit from this series. For example, a football athletic trainer may need to provide medical care for a local gymnastics meet. Although the emergency medical principles and action plan would remain the same, the athletic trainer could provide better care for the gymnasts after reading a simple overview of the principles of gymnastics in *Sports Injuries*.

Although these books offer an overview, they are not intended to be comprehensive in the recognition and management of sports injuries. The text helps the reader appreciate and gain awareness of the common injuries possible during participation in sports. Reference material and directed readings are provided for those who want to delve further into the subject.

Written in a direct and easily accessible style, *Sports Injuries* is an enjoyable series that will help young people learn about sports and sports medicine.

Susan Saliba, Ph.D., National Athletic Trainers' Association Education Council

The American figure skater Sarah Hughes performs at the 2002 U.S. National Figure Skating Championships.

History

How long have humans been ice skating? Well, the oldest pair of skates found so far are some 5,000 years old and were made around 3000 B.C.E. Found at the bottom of a lake in Switzerland, the blades were made from the bones of large mammals.

The earliest skaters made holes at each end of these long bones and then used thick leather straps made from animal skins to attach the bones to their feet. Later, skates were made from polished wood.

At some point in the fourteenth century, Europeans began fixing flat iron "runners," or facings, to the bottom, making the skates stronger and giving them better movement on the ice. Until the sixteenth century, skaters used poles to steer and propel themselves. Then the introduction of a double-edged metal blade, which gave the skate grip on the ice, meant that skaters could use the skate itself for steering and propulsion. This skating action was known as the "Dutch roll."

Later, the sport of skating was introduced to the Americas by Europeans, and technological advances were soon being made. In Philadelphia in 1848, a man named E. V. Bushnell invented the first all-steel clamp for skates, which quickly became very popular. The steel was lighter than other material and less corrodible, and also provided a tighter fit for the skate. Then, in 1865, Jackson Haines, a famous American skater, came up with the idea for a two-plate, all-metal blade. This blade

Skating has been a favorite pastime for many years, as this old photograph of a flamboyantly dressed female figure skater demonstrates.

ICE SKATING

JACKSON HAINES

Known as the American Skating King, Jackson Haines revolutionized figure skating in the nineteenth century. Jackson was born in Troy, New York, in 1840, a time when style and dancelike grace were virtually unknown on the skating rink. Jackson changed all that, studying dance and then bringing dance routines accompanied by music into figure skating. He also changed the design of skates and invented the toe pick.

The winner of the U.S. men's championship, Jackson pioneered a unique approach to the sport, which became known as the "International Style." It was not universally popular in his lifetime—he died in Europe in 1875—but it eventually became the accepted approach to modern skating. For that reason, Jackson Haines can truly be called the father of modern figure skating.

was fixed directly to Haines' boots. This provided greater precision and firmness for the skater and is still the basic model used for skates today. In the 1870s, Haines added the first **toe pick**, which made it possible to perform toe pick jumps. Another major breakthrough in skating came early in the twentieth century, when John E. Strauss, from St. Paul, Minnesota, invented the first closed toe blade made from a single piece of steel. This not only made the skates stronger, but lighter as well.

DIFFERENT TYPES OF SKATING

Skating falls into two broad categories—figure skating and speed skating. Both forms are part of traditional winter games and are featured in the Winter Olympics.

HISTORY

Figure skating involves skaters performing a variety of spins, jumps, and set movements across a rink. Two offshoots from this are synchronized skating and ice dance. This last, as its name suggests, combines skating and dancing.

Figure skating is both an individual sport and a "team" sport, in which pairs of skaters compete. At its best, figure skating demands great technical skill on the part of the skater, though artistic interpretation of routines is increasingly important, too.

In speed skating, the emphasis is on sheer speed. This sport is divided into two main branches: **long track** and **short track**. Long track involves two skaters on the track competing for time over distances of 545–10,940 yards. (500–10,000 m). In the United States and Canada, "pack style" long track racing involves up to eight skaters competing on the track, not confined to lanes. In the newer sport of short track speed skating, competitors race directly against each other.

SKATING AT THE OLYMPICS

Figure skating was an event at the very first Winter Olympics, which was held in 1924 at Chamonix in

The Norwegian-born Sonja Henie (1912–1969) was one of the early superstars of figure skating, winning three gold medals in the Winter Olympic Games of 1928, 1932, and 1936.

ICE SKATING

JUMPS

- **The axel**—the skater takes off from the forward inside edge of the blade and turns one and a half times while in the air, then lands on the back outside edge of the opposite blade.
- **The double axel**—an axel in which the skater turns two and a half times while in the air.
- **The flip**—using the toe pick at the front of the skate to help, the skater takes off from the back inside edge of one skate and lands on the back outside edge of the opposite skate.
- **The loop**—the skater takes off from and lands on the same back outside edge of the skate.
- **Edge jumps**—any jump in which the skater takes off from an edge of the foot without using the power of the other foot.
- **The Salchow**—an edge jump where the skater takes off from the back inside edge of one foot, then makes a full turn to land on the back outside edge of the other.

The American figure skater Dick Button is shown here on the eve of the Oslo Winter Olympic Games in 1952.

France. The Olympics feature four figure skating events: the men's singles, the women's singles, the mixed pairs, and mixed ice dancing.

The singles events have two sections: the short program and **free skating**. The short program consists of eight compulsory elements, including jump combinations and spins. For free skating, skaters perform an original arrangement of techniques to music of their choice.

As with the singles, the pairs event also has a short program section and a free skating section. The couple are expected to work as one unit, showing not just technical skill, but also harmony and grace.

U.S. speed skater Charles Jewtraw became the first person to win a gold medal in any Winter Olympic competition when he won the 500-meters (545-yd) speed skating race at Chamonix, France, in 1924.

Ice dancing, on the other hand, is more like ballroom dancing, and the emphasis in this particular competition is on performing the complex steps in time with the music.

The ice dancing event has three sections—compulsory, original, and free dances. In compulsory dancing, the couple performs two pre-determined dances. Original dances must follow specified rhythms, though the pair are allowed to choose their own music. In the free dancing section, the couple can express themselves freely when interpreting their chosen music.

ICE SKATING

APOLO ANTON OHNO

Apolo Ohno has proved himself one of the brightest stars in the rapidly growing sport of short track speed skating. Born in 1982 and raised in Seattle, Washington, Apolo has risen quickly to become both an Olympic gold medalist and a World Cup winner—not bad for someone who began speed skating only in 1995 when he was thirteen. An immensely powerful athlete, Apolo became the youngest American to win a World Cup event at the age of seventeen. He was the 1,500-m (1,640 yd) gold medal winner at the 2002 Olympics and overall champion at the 2001 World Cup.

SPEED SKATING

Speed skating became part of the first Winter Olympics in 1924, though women's events were not held until 1960. At the Olympics, the longer form of speed skating consists of ten events. These are the 500 meters (545 yd), 1,000 meters (1,090 yd), 1,500 meters (1,640 yd), and 5,000 meters (5,470 yd) for both men and women, plus the 3,000 meters (3,280 yd) for women and the grueling 10,000 meters (10,940 yd) for men. The distances are skated once, except for the two 500-meter (545-yd) events, which are skated twice.

In all the events, the competitors race in pairs against the clock, with their times recorded down to one-hundredth of a second. In the case of the 500-meter (545-yd) events, the skater's two times count toward the final result.

Competitors skate counterclockwise around the track, and each lane is divided by **markers**. Because the inside lane is shorter than the outside lane, competitors

HISTORY

must change lanes during each lap to make sure that they skate the same distance. This is done at the **crossover** point in the backstretch—the skater crossing the outer lane to the inner lane has the right of way. The skater starting in the inner track wears a white armband; the skater starting in the outer lane wears a red one. Skaters can be disqualified for having two false starts; for crossing the lane markers while in the bends; for failing to change lanes in the crossing area; and for interfering with an opponent when changing lanes.

Short track speed skating

Short track speed skating first appeared at the 1992 Winter Olympics, and, since then, speed skaters have tended to specialize in either long or short track.

The key difference with short track events is that competitors race against each other, not against the clock, as in the longer form. This means that racing tactics and techniques come into play. Four skaters take part at a time, and those coming in first and second place go on to the next round.

U.S. speed skater Eric Heiden made history at the 1980 Lake Placid Winter Games when he became the first Olympian to win five individual gold medals.

These heats reduce the number of competitors until the final, when the rule is simple; the first to cross the finish line is the winner. As with track athletics, the winning time is less important than coming in first.

At the Olympics, short track speed skating consists of eight events. Men and women take part in 500-meter (545-yd), 1,000-meter (1,090-yd), and 1,500-meter (1,640- yd) races, while there is a 5,000-meter (5,470-yd) relay for men, and a 3,000-meter (3,280-yd) relay for women. The men's and women's short track relays are two-day events made up of a semifinal and a final. Eight teams are split into two heats of four. The top two teams in each semifinal go on to the final.

SKATING RINKS AND COURSES

In figure skating, ice rinks must be 200 feet long and 100 feet wide (60.9 x 30.4 m) for Olympic events, though domestic competition rinks can measure 185 x 85 feet (56.3 x 25.9 m).

In the longer form of speed skating, skaters compete around a standard 440-yard (400-m) oval course. Short track speed skating takes place on a 121-yard (111-m) oval track. The corners are very tight, and it can be difficult for skaters to maintain control. Therefore, surrounding boards must be covered by protective mats of polyurethane foam, which are at least 8 inches (20 cm) thick and 39 inches (1 m) high. The mats are covered with a water-resistant and cut-resistant material and are attached to the boards, as well as to each other.

- The hardness of ice can vary in a rink or on a speed skating course, and this affects skating. When the ice is harder, the glides are longer, but the surface can break when you try to push on it. Softer ice makes it easier to get a grip, but slightly reduces the ease of glide.

HISTORY

KRISTI TSUYA YAMAGUCHI

Born in Freemont, California, in July 1971, Kristi Yamaguchi has enjoyed a remarkable career as a figure skater. Soon after she was born, Kristi needed surgery to correct a problem with her feet, and it was her mother who encouraged her to take up skating to strengthen her legs. Kristi worked hard at her skating, and by 1987 she had won two international junior titles. The following year, the young skater won the gold medal in the women's singles at the world junior championships. Four years later came her greatest achievement of all: winning the women's singles event at the Albertville Olympic Games in 1992, thus becoming the first American women skater to win an Olympic gold medal for sixteen years. In total, Kristi won fourteen out of twenty-one major championships between 1987 and 1992, winning the World Figure Skating Championship titles twice. Since the 1992 Olympics, Kristi has won a string of professional titles, and, in 1994–1995, she won the Best of the Best competition.

Kristi Yamaguchi skating for the gold medal at the 1992 Winter Games in Albertville, France.

Mental Preparation to Avoid Injury

Sports are often won or lost in the mind. Among top-class athletes, who all have great ability and technique, it is often the person with the best mental preparation who goes on to win. Just as importantly, such preparation also reduces the number of injuries.

The reason for this is simple. Injuries often occur when competitors are not sufficiently focused, or lack confidence in what they are doing. This can lead to poor technique, which for skaters can mean falls or tumbles under the pressure of competition. Good mental preparation will improve your performance and reduce the likelihood of injuries by ensuring that you are focused and that your technique is correct. And just as it is essential for competitions, it is essential for training, too.

MENTAL PREPARATION TECHNIQUES

One of the most important mental techniques is to use what is often called "imagery." You, the athlete, make a mental picture of what you are going to do during your performance. It has been said that nothing is either good or bad, but that "thinking makes it so." In the same way, if your mind is telling you that you are going to do badly in a sport, the chances are that you will indeed do badly. On the other hand,

Figure skater Beatrisa Liang, seen here at the State Farm U.S. Figure Skating Championship, shows the mental concentration essential for all successful skaters.

ICE SKATING

Swiss skating pair Daniel and Elaine Hugentobler, who are brother and sister, successfully complete a freestyle dance routine on the ice in the 2002 Winter Olympics in Salt Lake City.

if your mind is convinced you are going to do well, you have a much better chance of success. So it is important that before a skating event—and even before training—you imagine yourself doing your routines well. Here are a few tips:

- Imagine you are on the ice rink or at the race. You are aware of the noise, the crowds, and the other competitors, but are shutting all that out to concentrate on your performance.
- Imagine yourself going through an entire race or routine, not just part of it. Visualize yourself doing each jump, turn, start, or bend—depending, of course, on what kind of skating event you are involved in.

- Tell yourself that each part of your performance will be excellent. Imagine yourself performing each technique correctly, with precision, with power, and with perfect timing.
- If you are preparing for a race, imagine yourself heading for the line, perhaps coming from behind or perhaps leading from the front—but, in each case, getting to the line first.
- If you have had an injury—in a leg or foot, for example—imagine yourself putting the strain on that leg or foot during the event and then finding that it's okay.
- Tell yourself that you will perform each part of your routine well, that you are relaxed and focused—and that you are going to do well.

If you can manage this, the winning should take care of itself! What's more, you should find that your increased confidence and self-awareness, as well as focus, will help you avoid many of the injuries associated with your event.

COACHES AND BOOKS

As well as using these simple mental techniques, it is important to consider other ways of helping yourself to perform and prevent injuries. You or your team may have a coach—and a good one will be able to help you a great deal. The coach will assess your technique and style, work on your speed and power, and advise you on small changes of technique or tactics that can help improve your performance. A coach is a valuable source of feedback on what you are doing right and what you are doing wrong. Sometimes it takes an outsider to spot your weaknesses and then help to correct them.

A coach should also help you improve your confidence. To do this, there needs to be mutual trust between you and your coach. Trust and confidence is a two-way thing. You need to listen and respect your coach's opinions, in the same way that your

ICE SKATING

While skaters certainly learn a lot from solitary practice, it is the advice of a hands-on coach that can make all the difference to your performance.

coach will listen to your views and comments. It can take a little time to build up this relationship, so work at it and make sure you fulfill your side of the bargain. Another crucial factor is honesty—honesty with yourself. You may not always like what your coach is saying—no one enjoys criticism—but you have to ask yourself if the criticism is fair. Deep down, you may know it is; if so, there is no point complaining about it! The one thing an athlete can never afford to do is to lie to himself.

It is also important that young skaters read books or watch instruction CDs, videos, and DVDs. Books may not be as useful as having a coach—they cannot show you if

MENTAL PREPARATION TO AVOID INJURY

TACTICS DURING SPEED SKATING

The short track speed skater needs to be smart as well as speedy. Competitors race against each other, not the clock, so timing your finish is crucial. Some racers prefer to lead from the front and set a fast pace, hoping that their strength and fitness will wear down the rest of the skaters. Another tactic is to hold back just behind the front skaters, saving energy, and then to sprint for the line as the race draws to a close. A third tactic is to alternate between short sprints and hanging back, in the hope that this will disrupt a competitor's strategy.

In all cases, you should be within the leading two or three places with just four or five laps to go. Overtaking or passing—which requires great acceleration, balance, and agility—gets harder as the race draws to its climax. You are not allowed to push your opponents! The lead skater has the right of way, so it is the passer who must avoid any body contact. Intentionally pushing, blocking, or colliding with an opponent will lead to a disqualification.

U.S. competitor Dan Jansen, in action in the 500-m (545-yd) race at the 1988 Winter Olympic Games in Calgary, showing the raw power of speed skating.

FIGURE SKATING: GET A ROUTINE

U.S. figure skater Tara Lipinski shows her pleasure at getting it right during her routine at the 1998 Winter Olympics at Nagano, Japan.

Figure skating requires great discipline and focus from the skater to get the performance right. To help you to stay calm and focused, it is a good idea to develop a fixed routine or set of rituals before you perform. Sticking to this in the preparation for an event will help you to avoid distractions and will bring you calmness and confidence. Such a routine will include getting your regular amount of sleep before you compete; deciding what you eat and when; and choosing the time you arrive for a competition, how long it will take you to get changed, the amount of time you spend on warm-up, and the time you will spend on your mental preparation. Choose the time when you say goodbye to your friends and family, and from this point onward concentrate on you and what you want to achieve. Following the same routine each time will help you to gain control of yourself.

you are doing something wrong—but they can be a great source of information. And you can read and reread them until you have taken in all the information you need. There are a variety of books for young skaters, covering topics such as techniques, physical conditioning, and mental preparation. You cannot be expected to read them all, but find one that suits you and work with it.

And remember to be precise in the way that you follow techniques and suggestions. The old saying that "Practice makes perfect" is not entirely right; it should say "Perfect practice makes perfect."

THE DANGERS OF OVERCONFIDENCE

Finally, a brief word about being too confident. The mental exercises discussed here are intended to give you confidence, enabling you to believe in yourself and perform well. They will indeed help your performance—but they are not a substitute for the performance itself. We are all familiar with the sports team or individual who thought that turning up at the event was enough to secure a victory. And then, against all expectations, came defeat. The point is, you have to earn your win by your performance on the rink or track. So, when you prepare mentally, you must remember to concentrate on your performance, not on the medal you may win.

U.S. figure skater Timothy Goebel, seen here at the U.S. Figure Skating Championship in 2001, demonstrates the mental determination and physical precision needed to be a top skater.

Warming Up to Avoid Injury

Many injuries in sports occur in the early stages of a competition. One of the reasons for this is the lack of proper physical preparation. Your body must be stretched, loose, and warmed up before starting any strenuous physical activity. You should concentrate especially on those parts of the body that will be exercised most by your event.

Warm-up is important at any time and is even more important in the morning when your muscles are at their coldest. The simple reason is this: when your muscles are cold, they are more brittle and have less elasticity than when they are warm. As a result, if your muscles are not properly warmed up, you are more likely to tear them.

This golden rule applies to every sport, and skating is certainly no exception. In figure skating events, for example, you have only a short period of warm-up time on the ice before a competition begins and you are putting your skills—and your muscles—to the test. It is therefore essential that your body is properly warmed up off-ice to reduce the risk of injury. Similarly, speed skating is an explosive discipline; if your body is not fully warmed up beforehand, you can end up injuring yourself, possibly seriously.

A good coach will help skaters in their warm-up routines so that the skater can avoid injury as well as improve his or her skating technique.

ICE SKATING

Top skaters such as Tara Lipinski, seen here warming up, know the importance of stretching their muscles before skating to avoid injury.

OFF-ICE WARM-UP

The first part of your warm-up routine off-ice should be a general **aerobic** workout. This means any form of exercise that will increase your heart rate and get the blood flowing around your body. It will also raise the core temperature of your muscles, ensuring that they are less likely to be damaged during your competition, and will help your body work at maximum level.

This aerobic exercise could take several forms. You might want to perform a slow jog, use a jumping rope, or do step-ups on a bench or box. Ideally, this exercise should last between around five and eight minutes. If you do it for much longer than this, you might begin to tire yourself out needlessly. If the time is much shorter, you may not be making your body work hard enough. Make sure that you have a comfortable pair of exercise shoes for this warm-up, and perform it in a safe and comfortable environment. Make sure, too, that you are free from distractions—this part of your routine is as important as every other part, and you have to take it seriously. Get into a regular routine with the form of aerobic exercise that suits you best.

Some people like to try sprints and even jumps at this time as well, but again you may find this tires you unnecessarily.

STRETCHING

The next, equally important part of your off-ice routine is stretching exercises. It is important for a skater to have good mobility. Too much tightness in your body before you compete can cause a variety of injuries, such as a pulled hamstring, sore back or knee, and ankle injuries.

These stretching exercises must be thorough, covering your entire body. It is a good idea to start at one end of your body and work methodically through to the other end—from head to toe, or from toe to head. Ideally, this routine should take around ten minutes.

Here is a selection of stretching exercises to perform. Try to hold the stretches for around ten to twelve seconds each:

It is important that you perform your stretching routines methodically, with slow, powerful movements.

ICE SKATING

Neck

Stand upright with your hands on your hips, and slowly rotate your head to stretch your neck muscles. Do complete circles in both directions—clockwise, then counterclockwise. Do not force it, but rotate your head in a slow and controlled fashion.

Arms and shoulders

1. Standing upright, hold your arms up and straight, then slowly rotate them in a circle. Again, do this in both directions, clockwise and counterclockwise, in a slow and controlled fashion.

2. Place one arm across your body and pull it toward you using the other arm. Repeat with the other arm. After this, link your hands together behind your body and pull them up toward the sky. Once again, do this in a slow and controlled manner. Hold the stretch.

Trunk

Standing upright, put your hands on your hips and slowly rotate your body around, first clockwise and then counterclockwise.

Hamstring

This is a very common but useful exercise. Cross

Ice skating routines involve a lot of twisting and turning: always loosen up the trunk of your body before beginning any on-ice work.

WARMING UP TO AVOID INJURY

Your calf muscles are vulnerable to pulls and strains, so it is important that they are as loose and supple as possible before you skate.

your legs, and, with your arms outstretched, slowly move your hands toward your toes. Hold the stretch. It is important that you do this slowly and that you do not bounce up and down—this can cause injury. Repeat this with your legs crossed in the other direction.

This exercise should reduce the chances of pulling a hamstring when you first go onto the ice.

Quadriceps

Standing up straight on one leg, grab one foot behind your buttocks. You should be able to do this without having to hold on to something or someone. Hold the position. Make sure that you repeat this with the other leg an equal number of times.

Calf stretch

The **calf muscle** is very important for a skater. If this part of your body is not properly loose before going on ice, it is easy to get a slight calf strain or even tear. For this exercise, stand up straight by a tree or wall, and place one foot against it. Keep your leg straight, and move your hips toward the tree or wall until you feel your calf stretch.

Shins

The shins are another important and sometimes neglected area for a skater. Stand upright, but with your knees slightly bent. Curl one knee behind the other. Point the toes on your front foot down toward the ground. Push on the front knee using the knee behind until you feel the stretch across your shin. Repeat the other way round.

Groin

Groin strains are a common problem for skaters, so make sure that you stretch this area carefully before any event. Sit up straight and then, easing your legs toward your body, place the soles of your feet together. Your knees should be eased out toward the floor. Put your elbows on the insides of your knees and slowly and

FAILURE TO WARM UP

If you do not warm up properly before skating, you have only yourself to blame if you suffer an injury as a result. The most common types of injury resulting from failure to warm up include strained hamstrings, calf muscles, and groins. If you are really unlucky, you might pull a calf muscle or hamstring. These sort of injuries may not seem serious, but, remember, they can put you out of action for weeks. In many cases, the only real "cure" is rest. If you continue to perform or train with such problems, you will eventually be forced to stop for even longer. If you think that you have seriously pulled a muscle, you should always seek expert medical advice.

U.S. figure skater Brian Boitano in 1988, the year he won the gold medal at the Calgary Olympics.

gently push your knees toward the ground. If you do not feel anything, bring your feet closer to your body.

Hips

Another important area to consider in your routine are your hips. Here, stand up and then lunge forward with one foot. Then push your pelvis forward until you feel your hip flexors stretching. Repeat this the other way round.

These two stretches, as well as the seated groin stretch above, are very important if you will be doing starts or sprints.

GENERAL ADVICE

When performing these routines, it is a good idea to find an area which has some matting or other soft surface. The last thing you will want to do is to pick up unnecessary bruises or bumps from a hard surface before you perform.

Give yourself some time, about ten to fifteen minutes, between the end of your warm-up and going onto the ice. You do not want to have to rush at this point to lace up your skates, and you need time to refocus your mind on the skating ahead of you. Make sure that you do not get cold during this interval—put on warm clothing and do not sit still for too long. Keep your arms and legs moving, if possible.

ON-ICE WARM-UP

Once you are on the ice, it is important to perform some specific warm-up routines. This means carrying out exercises that mimic exactly the kind of activity you will be performing in the event or race to come. There are two reasons for doing this. First, the exercises get your body prepared for the exertions ahead, which will greatly reduce your chance of injury. Second, the on-ice warm-up will get you mentally prepared for the challenge ahead.

The precise exercises you perform will depend on your sport and your ability. A figure skater might perform a set number of ankle bounces, single **axel** jumps, or floor landing positions. The speed skater might perform some starts and some short sprints. It is important to perform these actions with precision, just as you would in the real thing. At the same time, it is important not to tire yourself out with too many repetitions. A five- to ten-minute on-ice warm-up is sufficient.

COOL-DOWN

The cool-down period after a race or routine is as important as the warm-up before it. If you can stay on ice after the event, spend a few minutes gently skating, during which time you should feel your heart rate gradually decreasing.

After you have taken off your skates, try a few stretches, as in the warm-up exercises. However, do not stretch if you feel you have pulled or torn any muscles—you could make things worse. Afterward, and especially if you have not had enough time on ice to cool down, you can go for a slow jog.

The cool-down helps your body to pump blood away from the major muscles used for skating (especially in the legs) and into your major organs, such as your heart and lungs. It also helps to reduce the waste material produced by your muscles during exercise—lactic acid. Reducing lactic acid levels can reduce exhaustion, fatigue, and stress.

Equipment

The equipment you need depends on your type of skating. In figure skating, your skates are by far the most important piece of equipment. In speed skating, other items become important, particularly in short track speed skating, where the competitive nature of racing makes safety equipment essential.

For all skating, the essential tool is, of course, the skate. You must make sure that the skate is right for you—ill-fitting skates, whether too big or too small, can cause problems for your feet and lower legs. Some of the equipment you will need is not cheap, so look after it properly to ensure that it lasts for as long as possible. And remember, buying very inexpensive equipment is not always the best solution, because cheap products can wear out more quickly.

FIGURE SKATING
Boots

Olympic figure skaters wear boots that are custom-made for each foot and reinforced with thick, stiff leather interiors and extra ankle bracing. In general, skating boots do not allow much movement of the foot once they are laced up, so it is important to make the right choice of boot. For your feet to feel comfortable, the texture of the boot should be neither too stiff nor too soft. Your foot should fit snugly inside the skate once it is tied, to give you maximum control over the skate, but should not feel so tight that you are uncomfortable. Nor do you want your feet to be able to

For any skater, whether you are into speed or figure skating, the essential tool of your sport is your skate.

To get the maximum speed and traction from your skates, the blades must be kept in the best possible condition.

move around too much inside the boot because this will cause blisters and will reduce your precision while skating. You should also do strengthening exercises for your feet and lower legs, so that your boots do not cause you any pain or injury.

Cheaper boots come with blades already attached. With better quality boots and skates, it is normal to buy them separately.

Blades

A modern figure skating blade has a very slight curve, based on a radius of 70–86 inches (180–220 cm). The blade is sharpened to produce a flat, or concave, cross-section. To maintain a sharp edge, the bottom $1/4$ inch (6 mm) of the blade is made from tempered steel. Different blades skate differently—those for advanced skaters offer more freedom and movement, which may be too much for the beginner. Always make sure that you find a blade that suits your ability.

Skating wear

The most important factors are that the outfits are comfortable to wear; that they enable full freedom of movement; and that they are light and durable enough to withstand those inevitable falls on the ice.

CARING FOR YOUR BOOTS AND BLADES

Boots and blades are the most expensive equipment for a figure skater. Make sure that you dry your boots and blades properly after you have finished skating.

EXTRA PADDING FOR FIGURE SKATERS

For many years, figure skaters simply had to put up with the occasional bumps and bruises that come from falls. Now, however, there are a number of products that help to protect the skater. These include knee pads, butt pads, pads to protect the back, wrist guards to help prevent arm fractures, and pads to stop the rubbing of boots. These new pads are made of strong, light, shock-absorbing material, and many of them are surprisingly unobtrusive and comfortable to wear. Their advantage is that they can give the beginning skater the confidence to try new things and make mistakes, knowing that a fall will not be too painful. It is also a good idea for novice skaters to wear helmets on the ice while they build up confidence.

Water will rust the blades and damage the boots. Once rusted, a blade will have to be replaced because it cannot be sharpened properly.

Do not store the blades in the hardened guard you use for wearing the blades off the ice. This guard will hold in the moisture. Instead, keep the blade in a "soaker," a soft guard that draws away excess moisture from the metal.

Keep your blades well sharpened; you will know they need this when you begin skidding sideways! If you skate every day, you will probably have to sharpen your blades about every five weeks. Be very careful when handling your blades, especially when removing the excess ice from them after a workout.

SPEED SKATING
Boots and blades

For speed skaters, caring for the boot and blade is much the same as for figure skaters. With a speed skate, the part of the blade that comes in contact with the ice forms a straight line.

For men, speed skating blades are generally 16–18 inches (42–46 cm) long; for women, blades may be as short as 12 inches (30 cm).

Beginners can usually begin with figure skating or hockey skates while

The great American speed skater Bonnie Blair warms up on the ice before a competition at the 1992 Winter Olympic Games.

CLAP SKATES

Clap skates became popular in the 1998 Nagano Winter Olympics in Japan and are now used by all top long-track speed skaters. They have dramatically speeded up skating times, although some critics have their reservations: this is an innovation that is not used outside the world of competitive racing. Unlike conventional skates, the heel of the clap-skate blade is not attached to the boot, while the toe of the blade is fastened to the boot with a hinged apparatus. At the end of each stride, as the skater picks up the skate, the blade briefly disconnects from the heel of the boot. This leaves the blade resting on the ice a bit longer, increasing the skater's pushing power. When the blade has fully extended, a spring mechanism mounted on the front of the boot automatically snaps the blade back up to the boot, resulting in the "clapping" sound that gives the skate its name.

they see if they like the sport. These skates do not offer the speed or performance of the longer speed skates, but it makes more sense to use them until you have decided whether or not speed skating is for you—speed skates are expensive.

Other equipment

Many speed skaters wear goggles, which help to protect their eyes from the wind, as well as from ice chips thrown up by other competitors. The lenses also reduce the sun's glare on the ice and can help improve visibility. Serious racers also wear skin-tight racing suits with hoods to reduce air drag.

SHORT TRACK SPEED SKATING

As a safety measure, the short track form of speed skating requires you to have more safety equipment. Serious injuries are rare, but it is a good idea to make sure you are properly protected.

Helmets

All skaters must wear some kind of hard-shelled helmet to protect against falls and the skates of other racers. For beginners, cycling helmets or hockey helmets are generally fine. When you become more serious about racing, you can upgrade to a specially-made skating helmet. Such helmets are very light, but tough.

Neck guards

These are very important because they protect the vulnerable neck and upper chest areas. They have been required for short track speed skating in Canada for a number of years and in the United States and at international competitions since 1996. They must be of the "bib" style, which gives protection to the chest as well as the neck.

Hockey neck guards are often worn. The guard should tuck inside the skin suit, so make sure it is the right size and comfortable to wear.

Knee pads and shin pads

Knee pads guard against hard falls as well as the skates of other racers. Also a good idea are shin protectors, and fortunately these are inexpensive. Similar to pads worn by soccer players, they fit snugly around a skater's shins, an area that can receive some very painful blows. Calf protectors are also often worn with knee and shin pads, offering total protection of the lower leg.

EQUIPMENT

Gloves

All skaters will need to wear some form of gloves to prevent cuts from contact with skate blades, or grazes from contact with the ice. In some competitions, non-knit gloves are required because these give better protection.

Long sleeves

Do not go onto the ice wearing a short-sleeved shirt or, even worse, short pants. Long-sleeved shirts and long pants give essential protection and comfort. Many skaters wear Lycra outfits, and others wear all-in-one skin suits, often made from spandex. Always make sure that you are warm enough when you are out practicing in the cold. If necessary, take some warm clothing to put on over your skating outfit while you are waiting around.

Skates

As with long track skating, you may initially want to try out short track racing with figure skating or hockey skates. Figure skates have a better shape for speed skating than hockey skates, but you run the risk of snagging a toe pick when you lean over in a turn. Hockey skates do not have this problem, but the blade's shape can lead to poor technique.

For stability and durability, the short track skate has a heavier construction than the long track version.

Dutch speed skater Marianne Timmer, who won the gold medal in the 1,000 meters (1.090 yd) during the 1998 Winter Olympic Games in Nagano.

43

Common Injuries and Treatment

Skating is great fun and, on the whole, safe, especially if you wear the right equipment and follow the advice of your coach. However, it is sensible to be aware of the kind of injuries you may suffer and how to prevent them, how to treat them, and how long it might take to recover from them.

It may seem a pretty obvious thing to say, but most of the injuries associated with figure skating are due to falling on the ice. So, before we look at some of the different injuries involved, let us consider the best way to fall. This is not as odd as it sounds: one of the certainties of figure skating is that you are going to fall. Most of the time, you will suffer nothing more than a slightly bruised ego! Occasionally, however, you might suffer a more serious injury, so learning how to fall the right way will reduce this risk.

If you think you are about to fall, it is often best to go ahead and let it happen. Struggling against the fall can make the resulting tumble even harder. The worst type of falls are those we fail to see coming—we can adjust to the ones we know are coming, and make them safer.

So how can you fall properly? Keep your head up as much as possible. If you are falling backward, tuck your chin into your chest so that you do not hit your

Accidents do happen in skating, even to the best; here, Russia's Anton Sikharulidze helps up Canadian Jamie Sale after accidentally crashing into her during a warm-up at the 2002 Salt Lake City Winter Games.

head on the ice. Try to keep your arms out of the way as you fall, because these are vulnerable to a sprain or a break. Admittedly, this is very difficult—it is instinctive to put your arms out to protect yourself. Also, try not to land on your knees, elbows, or tailbone, which are vulnerable to painful injuries. Instead, try to land on your thighs, hips, buttocks, and shoulders.

When you know that you are falling, bend your knees to get as low as possible, which will mean that there is less distance for your body to fall. Try to avoid falling over forward—your toe picks may catch in the ice. Also, when possible, try to "roll" with the fall to reduce the impact of landing on the ice. Once you get over your fear of falling, you will learn to fall better, making you more relaxed and less likely to suffer injury.

CONCUSSION

Perhaps the most dangerous type of injury you can suffer from a fall on the ice is concussion. If you do hit your head on the ice and feel dizzy and disoriented, or suffer even just a few moments of unconsciousness, you must leave the rink and make sure you get medical advice. You may not have a concussion, but you should not take any chances with this. If you have suffered a concussion, you should not venture back onto the ice until you have been given permission by a doctor. Rest is the cure, and this can take several weeks.

ARM INJURIES

Arm injuries are generally caused by skaters putting out their arms to protect against a fall. This is an instinctive reaction, and hitting the ice with your arm is, of course, better than hitting it with your head or face. Try to bend your elbow to reduce the stress on your arm.

COMMON INJURIES AND TREATMENT

FRACTURES

Wrist and arm fractures are one of the more common kind of breaks experienced by skaters. They usually occur when the skater uses an arm as protection during a fall. Often the break occurs to one of the two forearm bones, the ulna or the radius. Sometimes the fracture happens in the small navicular bone in the wrist, located just behind the thumb. This break is often a hairline fracture and is hard to detect with X-rays. The treatment of a wrist fracture depends on its exact location, stability, and on how many pieces of broken bone there are. Most are treated simply with a cast, but surgery is occasionally needed. These types of fractures can take at least six to eight weeks to heal.

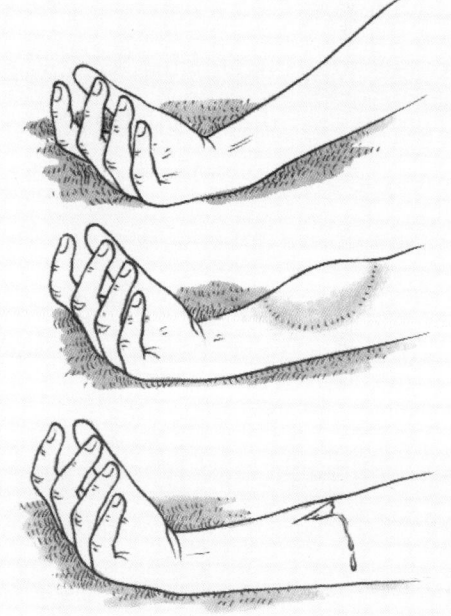

Fractures: The top drawing is of a normal arm, the middle shows a closed fracture, while the bottom image depicts an open fracture.

The most common injury you are likely to suffer is to your wrist. This will usually be a sprain, which can be painful and cause swelling. The main cure is rest, and recovery time can vary from days to a couple of weeks. Sometimes the swelling and pain will indicate that you have something more serious, such as a hairline fracture.

47

KNEE INJURIES

The knee obviously takes a lot of the strains during skating, both from falls and from the action of skating. Often a fall will result in simply a bruised knee, which is painful but can be treated by ice treatment and putting your feet up.

In very rare cases, a hard blow to the knee will cause misalignment of the knee cap, which can lead to chronic knee pain by wearing down of the knee cartilage. This condition is known as chondromalacia patellae. The best prevention is off-ice exercises to strengthen leg muscles.

If you twist your knee—for example, by landing badly after a jump—you can hurt the knee ligaments. Often the damage is to the medial collateral ligament (**M.C.L.**). This is associated with pain on the inner side of the knee and sometimes a feeling of instability in the knee. Complete rupture of this ligament could keep you off the ice for weeks, although this type of injury usually heals well with physical therapy. However, damage to the anterior cruciate ligament (**A.C.L.**)—at the front of the knee below the knee cap—often requires surgery. If you feel your knee "giving out" when you put weight on it, this may indicate you have torn the A.C.L. If in doubt, seek medical advice.

KNEE ANATOMY

The knee is one of the most vulnerable joints in the body. This diagram shows the front view of a flexed knee.

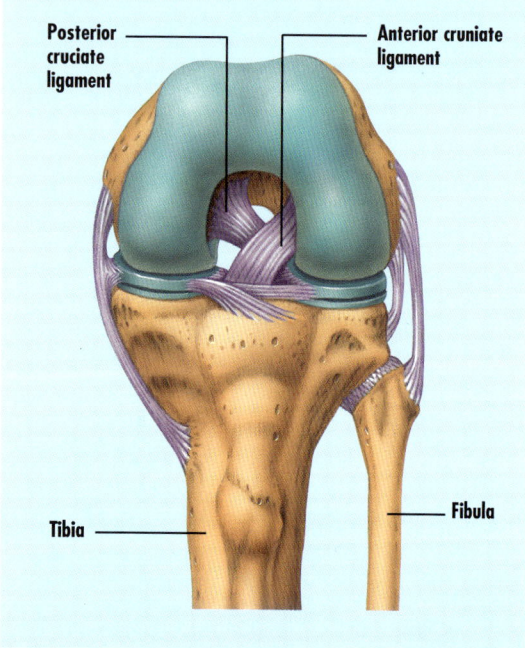

COMMON INJURIES AND TREATMENT

FOOT INJURIES

Foot pain is often caused by boots that are laced too tightly over the instep. The lacing should be tight, but not so tight that it cuts off circulation or hurts the foot. If your boots feel too tight even when the lacing is loosened, have the fit checked by an expert. Beginning skaters sometimes clench their toes while skating, which can cause the foot to cramp. This may be caused by boots that are too loose, keeping your weight too far forward on the blade, or may just be a bad habit.

The common foot problem that affects skaters is **plantar fasciitis**, a form of tendonitis that affects the soles of the feet, usually the heel. The standard treatment includes rest and anti-inflammatory drugs.

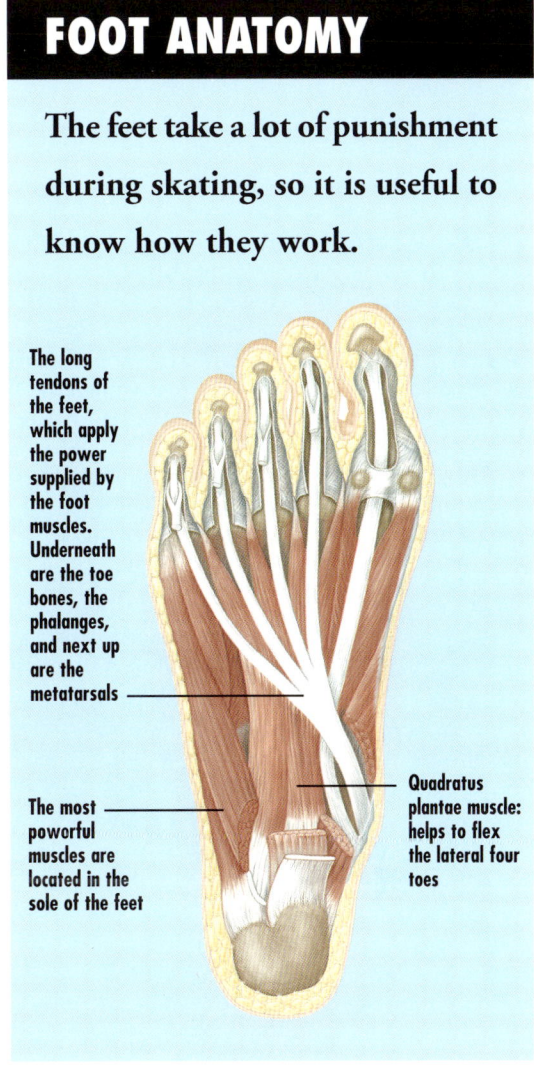

FOOT ANATOMY

The feet take a lot of punishment during skating, so it is useful to know how they work.

The long tendons of the feet, which apply the power supplied by the foot muscles. Underneath are the toe bones, the phalanges, and next up are the metatarsals

The most powerful muscles are located in the sole of the feet

Quadratus plantae muscle: helps to flex the lateral four toes

OVERUSE INJURIES

A lot of injuries, especially for experienced skaters, are "overuse injuries." These occur when the back, knees, legs, feet, or ankles suffer wear and tear from repeated exercises. Figure skating can put a great deal of strain on the hips. Tendonitis of the knees and lower leg is also common. This problem can be aggravated by

ICE SKATING

SPEED SKATING CUTS

The sharpness of speed skaters' blades and the ferocity of competition do make cuts a hazard, though correct padding reduces much of the risk. Common areas for cuts are the lower leg, ankles, hands, and arms. Cuts can look dramatic, but with correct, swift treatment, they should not keep a skater off the ice too long. The first actions are to stem the flow of blood with clean material and to call for medical help. Depending on the depth, length, and location of the cut, a doctor will probably apply stitches to close the wound.

Although blades are a skater's best friend, their sharpness means that they can cause deep cuts to the body; however, these injuries often look worse than they are.

COMMON INJURIES AND TREATMENT

Even the best skaters can fall, so it is wise to be prepared. Nancy Kerrigan (pictured) went on to win a silver medal in the 1994 Winter Olympics in Norway.

training while fatigued, or by skaters attempting techniques for which they are not yet ready. Apart from rest, other ways of preventing such overuse injuries include varying your routine, and off-ice strengthening exercises for the affected parts of your body. The right kind of physical conditioning and strengthening off the ice can save your body a great deal of stress on it.

Skaters also suffer from pulled or strained calf muscles and hamstrings. These are very often caused by failure to warm up properly, or by training when overtired. The only real cure is rest, which may range from a few days to many weeks, depending on severity.

Speed skating

In speed skating, many of the injuries are the same as for figure skating, including overuse injuries, concussion from falls, and wrist fractures. However, the hips and back are also vulnerable to overuse injuries because of the way skaters crouch low to reduce wind resistance. Racing against other competitors, especially in short track skating, also means that speed skaters are at risk of collisions. In addition to cuts, speed skaters can suffer neck and head injuries and dislocated shoulders because of the speed at which they travel during races.

Careers in Skating

At the moment, it is figure skating that offers skaters the richest variety of careers. Skaters remain eligible for competitions such as the Olympics, while also being able to earn money from professional shows, endorsements, and sponsorship.

The most high-profile careers are, of course, for the well-known performers such as U.S. figure skater Kristi Yamaguchi. Kamaguchi won Olympic gold in 1992 before going on to enjoy a successful professional career, skating in a series of shows and competitions.

However, the sport offers many career opportunities for skaters whose talents lie in other, more specialist roles. These include coaching; rink management; administration in rinks, clubs, or associations; education; sports science; medicine; off-ice conditioning; sports safety; and magazine publishing. Boot and blade technicians and manufacturers are also needed.

If you are seeking a career in the sport, it is up to you to find the right path. There are a variety of routes. These include training, testing, competing, apprenticing, educational courses via the Professional Skaters Association, or perhaps college courses in anatomy, physiology, biomechanics, physics, psychology, core body strength, human development, and other related fields.

Career opportunities in speed skating, which is a smaller but fast-growing sport

This is the moment that makes all the hard work worthwhile. U.S. figure skater Timothy Goebel stands on the podium after winning gold at the 2001 U.S. Figure Skating Championships.

at present, are more limited. Active world-class skaters, in the top five of their country in either long track or short track, are usually able to secure some type of sponsorship.

There are also a small but growing number of opportunities to move into a paid coaching position with a facility, a national governing body, a commercial team, or a private team. There are fifty or more full-time coaching positions in North America alone. Other career options include teaching physical education or facility management and program development for both elite and recreational skaters. People with these careers often get their start in coaching.

American figure skater Nancy Kerrigan performs a routine during the 2000 Goodwill Games in Lake Placid, New York.

COLLEGES AND SCHOLARSHIPS

With such a wide list of options for figure skating, you can see that any college offering an associate or four-year degree would be helpful. In addition, courses in business administration, computers, and bookkeeping are also helpful in the administrative areas. The University of Delaware has a four-year degree in Figure Skating and the United States Sports Academy in Daphne, AL, offers graduate courses for athletes. In addition, many colleges have their own figure skating or synchronized skating

CAREERS IN SKATING

The growing popularity of figure skating means that there are more career opportunities than ever, including coaching as well as performing.

teams. Most of these teams are student-run team sports on campus, so there is no scholarship money available specifically for figure skating. Remember, though, that whether you are a lone skater or a member of a Varsity Figure Skating Team, you can still compete at the National Collegiate Championships.

As Carole Shulman, Executive Director of the Professional Skaters Association says, "Figure skating offers many career choices and great opportunities in varied fields. The best advice for career success is to begin training in the sport, learning all you can about testing and competing. Simultaneously develop outside interests in related fields, where you can apply your figure skating background and experience. You do not need to actively perform on the ice in order to enjoy a long and successful career."

In speed skating, there is a scholarship available for students via the Amateur Speedskating Union (ASU) Foundation Scholarship Fund. Details can be found at www.speedskating.org.

For degree programs related to speed skating, one of the best institutions to investigate is the University of Calgary. The school has a faculty of kinesiology, as well as one of the top speed skating facilities in the world—the Calgary Olympic Oval, built for the 1988 Winter Olympic Games—right on its campus.

CAREERS AND INJURIES

If you are looking for a career in skating, one of the key requirements will be for you to stay as fit and injury-free as possible. No matter how talented you are, you will find it hard going if your body is unable to take the tough physical demands of the sport.

This means not just practicing your sporting technique, but also off-ice conditioning to strengthen joints and muscles, and to improve your aerobic

CAREERS IN SKATING

fitness. Make sure that you follow all the proper safety advice and wear the proper equipment. Remember, too, to eat a healthy, balanced diet.

Coping with injury

Olympic gold medal figure skater Tara Lipinski, who was born in 1982, had a meteoric rise to fame as one of the best skaters the United Sates has ever produced. But even while she was winning Olympic gold in 1998, Tara knew that something was not right with her hip, which had been causing her pain. She had been training and competing hard ever since she started skating at age six, and the wear and tear had taken its toll. Eventually she realized that something was seriously wrong—she had a torn hip muscle, or labrum. What's more, she knew that her career was over

Like any skater, Bonnie Blair, pictured in action here, had her share of injuries, but avoided serious setbacks because of her mental toughness and training routine.

57

INJURY-FREE DEREK PARRA

U.S. speed skater Derek Parra, who won a gold medal at the Salt Lake City Olympic Games in 2002, has battled against hip and back strain, as many top speed skaters do because of the way in which they bend low to stay streamlined. But the former inline skater, born in 1970, has helped keep serious injury at bay thanks to regular chiropractic care. Derek believes it is this brand of medicine—which involves the manipulation of the spinal column—that has kept him relatively pain-free. So much so, in fact, that the champion speed skater has been sponsored by the American Chiropractic Association (ACA). As Derek says: "I've used a lot of other treatments for injuries and pain, but the problem doesn't get fixed until I go to a doctor of chiropractic."

without a major operation. Fortunately, the operation was a success, and, although Tara does not skate competitively any more, she does still take part in ice shows. As she once said, "I couldn't imagine my life without skating."

Figure skater Michelle Kwan, who was born in 1980 in Torrance, California, and who later moved to Lake Arrowhead, became the first U.S. skater to win three World titles since Peggy Fleming, but had to fight against injury in 1997. In her first serious injury, she suffered a stress fracture of the second toe in her left foot. This made it very painful for her when she jumped. Although the Olympic Games were only three months away, Michelle was told by a doctor to put the foot in a cast and stay off the ice for three weeks. "Forcing myself not to skate took a lot more courage than anything I'd done till then. I was dying to get on the ice," said Michelle. But she followed the medical advice and was glad she did. In 1998, she came in first in nine major championships and second at the Olympics.

The great U.S. speed skater Bonnie Blair endured her fair share of pain, but during her remarkable career stayed sufficiently injury-free to win gold medals at three successive Olympic Games. Blair—nicknamed Bonnie the Blur—won the first of her five Olympic golds in 1988 and her last in 1994. She was also a member of the 1984 Olympic team, at age twenty. Bonnie's ability to stay relatively free from serious injury in this most grueling of sports is probably due to the fact that she was a great technician and was also blessed with a tremendous mental toughness, which enabled her to train hard and well. She is now a motivational speaker.

The glamorous American figure skater Michelle Kwan, shown in typical pose here, overcame serious injury to claim a silver medal at the 1998 Olympics in Japan.

Glossary

A.C.L.: The anterior cruciate ligament, which is situated at the front of the knee below the knee cap.

Aerobic: Exercise that demands increased oxygen, acquired by speeding up the heart rate and breathing.

Axel: A difficult figure skating jump, in which the skater takes off from the forward inside edge and lands on the back outside edge of the opposite skate. It is named for Scandinavian skater Axel Paulson, who invented it around the end of the nineteenth century.

Calf muscles: The muscles at the back of the lower leg, including the gastrocnemius and soleus; this group of muscles are particularly prone to injury among ice skaters.

Crossover: A technique of turning corners and gaining speed, in which the skater crosses one foot over the other.

Free skating: The part of the competition, typically four minutes long, when the skater performs movements to music.

Hamstrings: The group of three muscles set at the back of the thigh.

Long track: Speed skating competition in which two skaters at a time race against the clock on a 400-m. (440-yd.) track.

Marker: A plastic block that shows the boundary between lanes in speed skating. There are seven track markers at each bend.

Glossary

M.C.L.: The medial collateral ligament, on the inside of the knee.

Plantar fasciitis: An injury that affects the soles of the feet; it is caused by an inflammation of the plantar fascia muscles.

Quadriceps: A large four-part muscle on the front of the thigh, which is used to extend the leg.

Short track: Speed skating competition held on a 111-m. (121-yd.) track in an international-size hockey rink.

Toe pick: The teeth at the front of each skate blade, used by skaters to help with spins and jumps.

Further Information

USEFUL WEB SITES

Amateur Speedskating Union: www.speedskating.org

International Skating Union: www.isu.org

Olympic Games: www.olympic.org/uk/index_uk.asp

For biographies of skating stars: www.skatelog.com/skaters/artistic-ice

Speed Skating Canada: www.speedskating.ca

U.S. Figure Skating Online: www.usfsa.org/index.htm

U.S. Speedskating: www.usspeedskating.org

The Web sites listed on this page were active at the time of publication. The publisher is not responsible for Web sites that have changed their address or discontinued operation since the date of publication. The publisher will review and update the Web sites upon each reprint.

FURTHER READING

Boo, Michael. *The Story of Figure Skating.* New York: Beech Tree, 1998.

Foeste, Aaron and Bruce Curtis. *Ice Skating Basics.* New York: Cassell, 2000.

Morrissey, Peter and James Young. *Figure Skating School: A Professionally Structured Course from Basic Steps to Advanced Techniques.* London: Apple, 1997.

Poe, Carl M. *Conditioning for Figure Skating.* New York: Contemporary Books, 2002.

Publow, Barry. *Speed on Skates.* Champaign, Illinois: 1999.

U.S. Olympic Committee Sports Series. *A Basic Guide to Speed Skating.* Irvine, California: Griffin Publishing, 2002.

FURTHER INFORMATION

THE AUTHOR

Michael Streeter is a British-based writer and journalist who has written on subjects as diverse as sports, history, and gardening. A sports enthusiast, Michael is an avid skater and skier. As well as writing books, Michael is a former senior executive on a number of leading British national newspapers, including the *Independent on Sunday* and the *Daily Express*. He is married and lives in London.

THE CONSULTANTS

Susan Saliba, Ph.D., is a senior associate athletic trainer and a clinical instructor at the University of Virginia in Charlottesville, Virginia. A certified athletic trainer and licensed physical therapist, Dr. Saliba provides sports medicine care, including prevention, treatment, and rehabilitation for the varsity athletes at the University. Dr. Saliba holds dual appointments as an Assistant Professor in the Curry School of Education and the Department of Orthopaedic Surgery. She is a member of the National Athletic Trainers' Association's Educational Executive Committee and its Clinical Education Committee.

Eric Small, M.D., a Harvard-trained sports medicine physician, is a nationally recognized expert in the field of sports injuries, nutritional supplements, and weight management programs. He is author of *Kids & Sports* (2002) and is Assistant Clinical Professor of Pediatrics, Orthopedics, and Rehabilitation Medicine at Mount Sinai School of Medicine in New York. He is also Director of the Sports Medicine Center for Young Athletes at Blythedale Children's Hospital in Valhalla, New York. Dr. Small has served on the American Academy of Pediatrics Committee on Sports Medicine for the past six years, where he develops national policy regarding children's medical issues and sports.

Index

Page numbers in *italics* refer to photographs and illustrations.

accidents *see* injuries
aerobic training 28–9
Amateur Speedskating Union (ASU) 56
arm injuries 46–7

back injuries 58
blades 9–10, 38–40, *50*
Blair, Bonnie *40, 57, 59*
Boitano, Brian *33*
boots 37–41, 43, 49
Bushnell, E.V. 9
Button, Dick *12*

calf muscles 31, 32, 51
career development 53–9
clap skates 41
clothing 15, 39, 41, 43
coaches *26, 54, 55*
    importance 21–2
colleges 53, 54, 56
collisions *44*, 51
competitions 11, 13, 14–16, 23, 24, 27
concussion 46
courses 16
cuts 50

disqualification 15, 23
doctors 46, 50, 58

equipment *36*, 37–43, 50
exercises
    after injury 51
    cool-down 35
    range of movement 29–32, 34
    warm-up 26–35

falls 39, 45–8, *51 see also* injuries
figure skating 10–13, *20*, 24, 37–40, *51*
first aid 50
flexibility 29–32, 34
foot injuries 49
footwear 37–8, 39–40, 49
fractures 47, 58

Goebel, Timothy *25, 52*
goggles 41

Goodwill Games *54*
governing bodies 53, 56
groin 32, 34

Haines, Jackson 9–10
hamstring 30–1, 32, 51
head injuries 46
Heiden, Eric *15*
helmets 39, 42
Henie, Sonja *11*
hips 34, 49, 51, 57, 58
Hugentobler, Daniel and Elaine *20*

ice dancing 11, 13, *20*
ice skating *see* skating
injuries
    concussion 46
    fractures 47, 58
    hip 34, 49, 51, 57, 58
    knee 42, 48
    overuse 49, 51
    strains 32, 58

Jansen, Dan *23*
Jewtraw, Charles *13*
jumps 12, 13

Kerrigan, Nancy *51, 54*
knees 42, 48
Kwan, Michelle 58–9

legs 31, 32, 42, 51
Liang, Beatrisa *18*
Lipinski, Tara *24, 28, 57, 59*
long track skating 11, 14–15, 41

mats 16
mental preparation 19–25, 35
muscles
    developing 48
    flexibility 29–32, 34
    injuries 48, 51

neck 42

Ohno, Apolo *14*
Olympics *see* Winter Olympics
overuse injuries 49, 51

padding 39, 42, 50

pain 46, 47, 48
Parra, Derek 58
physical preparation 27–35, 51, 56–7
physical therapy 48
preparation
    mental 19–25, 35
    physical 27–35, 51, 56–7
Professional Skaters Association 53, 56
protective equipment 16, 39, 41–3, 50

rinks 16

safety equipment 16, 39, 41–3, 50
Sale, Jamie *44*
shins 32, 42
short track skating 11, 14, 15–16, 23
    safety measures 42–3
Sikharulidze, Anton *44*
skates 9–10, *36*, 37–41, 43, 49
skating
    origins 9–10
    see also figure skating; speed skating
speed skating 11, *13*, 14–16, 23, 40–1
    see also long track skating; short track skating
sponsorship 54
stretching 29–32, 34
surgery 47, 48, 58

Timmer, Marianne *43*
toe pick 10, 12, 46
training *see* preparation

U.S. Figure Skating Championships *18, 25, 52*
universities 53, 54, 56

visualization 19–21

warming up 24, 26–35, *44*
Winter Olympics 10
    figure skaters *12, 20, 24, 51*
    gold medallists *11, 13,* 14, *17, 43,* 53, 58, 59
    speed skating 16, *23, 40,* 41, 56
World Cup 14
World Figure Skating Championships 17, 58

Yamaguchi, Kristi *17,* 53